Chill

Author: Frizzell, Colin.
Reading Level: 6.4
Point Value: 6.0
Lexile Value: 820L
            Reading Counts

Chill

Colin Frizzell

orca soundings

Orca Book Publishers

Library and Archives Canada Cataloguing in Publication

Frizzell, Colin, 1971-

Chill / Colin Frizzell.

(Orca Soundings)

ISBN 1-55143-670-1 (bound) ISBN 1-55143-507-1 (pbk.)

I. Title. II. Series.

PS8611.R59C45 2006   jC813'.6   C2006-903258-0

Summary: How far will Chill and Sean go to expose a teacher's deception?

First published in the United States, 2006
Library of Congress Control Number: 2006928469

Orca Book Publishers gratefully acknowledges the support for its publishing
programs provided by the following agencies: the Government of Canada
through the Book Publishing Industry Development Program and the
Canada Council for the Arts, and the Province of British Columbia
through the BC Arts Council and the Book Publishing Tax Credit.

Cover design: Lynn O'Rourke
Cover photography: Getty Images

ORCA BOOK PUBLISHERS
PO Box 5626, STN. B
VICTORIA, BC CANADA
V8R 6S4

ORCA BOOK PUBLISHERS
PO Box 468
CUSTER, WA USA
98240-0468

www.orcabook.com
Printed and bound in Canada.

010 09 08 07 • 5 4 3 2

In memory of my dad, Art.

Acknowledgments

There are too many people to thank them all by name, so I'd like to give a blanket thanks to all my friends, family and the many teachers who encouraged and supported me along the way. Especially Dad (Art), who gave me a love of storytelling; Mum (Peggy), who gave me a love of words; and my sister, Trish, for her encouragement and endless proofreading.

Also I'd like to thank Andrew Wooldridge for taking a chance by giving me one.

Finally, and most importantly, thanks to my wife, Jordann, for her love, encouragement and patience.

"And these children that you spit on
As they try to change their worlds,
Are immune to your consultations,
They're quite aware
of what they're going through."
—David Bowie

Chapter One

Chill's foot dragged behind him like a murder victim being taken to a shallow grave by a killer too weak to do the job, but he still stood straighter than any other kid in school.

His presence far exceeded his wiry five-foot-nine, fifteen-year-old body. Chill's size didn't matter because he was fast, and the speed was made twice as powerful because no one expected it from a guy with a bum leg.

He held his head high and no one made fun of him. Well, except for that one kid.

It was back in grade five. He was a big guy, new to Glendale Elementary. Kids are like wolves when they arrive at a new school; they look for the weakest in the pack and try to take 'em down. This—they hope—will get them the much-needed acceptance of the pack. You can't survive in school on your own.

It was the first recess and the new kid, Shane or Wayne, something like that, spotted Chill. Once he saw Chill's leg, he made his move.

"Hey, hop-a-long," he called out, though Chill didn't hop. Hopping would have meant he was trying to appear normal, and Chill didn't try to be anything but what he was, and what he was, was Chill.

"Hop-a-long," the kid yelled out again.

Chill stopped. He shook his head like he'd been waiting for it. Like somehow he knew, from the moment he laid eyes on this kid, that it was going to come to this.

He sighed and turned but didn't say anything.

Chill wasn't much of a talker. He didn't have to be. His sharp eyes and multitude of expressions could speak volumes. On the other hand, I was a talker and often spoke for Chill.

"What do you want?" I said, sticking close to Chill's side.

"I'm not talking to you. I'm talking to Hoppy here," he said, nodding at Chill.

"I don't think he wants to talk to you," I told him.

"What's the matter?" he said. "His tongue as dead as his leg?"

The kid laughed. He looked around, hoping others would join him. No one did. He turned back to Chill.

"So what happened? Your leg fall asleep in class and you couldn't wake it up?" he laughed again and looked around again—nothing.

The lameness of the attempted jokes aside, he should have picked up on the lack of reaction from the crowd. He should have realized that no one appreciated what he was doing and that *this* wasn't going to gain him any friends.

Chill shook his head and turned to walk away.

"Where do you think you're going?" the kid asked. "Nowhere fast, that's for sure," he added.

As Chill walked away, so did everyone else.

The new kid was losing his audience. He grabbed Chill by the shoulder and spun him around. Chill lost his balance.

I went to catch him, but he caught himself before I could and straightened up proudly. Chill stared at the kid with a warning glare that would have made anyone with a lick of sense back off. This kid was not good at picking up on subtleties.

"You shouldn't walk away when people are talking to you," the kid threatened. "Didn't your mom teach you that? Or did she give up teaching you anything when she saw you couldn't even learn to walk?"

It took a lot for Chill to lose his cool, but it was definitely going. He turned away again. This time the kid swung Chill back around with all he had, determined to take him down.

But Chill was ready. He didn't so much spin as pirouette, with his bad leg swinging like a club.

Chill only meant to sweep his attacker's legs out from under him, but the kid had stiffened his leg so he could get the full momentum in his pull. When Chill's leg connected with the kid's knee, it gave a sickening pop that made everyone in the yard stiffen. The kid dropped like a gummy bear from the ceiling after the saliva dries.

Despite the pain, the kid tried to get to his feet to save face, but he could only move himself along the ground like a lame toad.

"Who's Hoppy now?" I yelled.

This got a laugh from everyone—except Chill.

When I turned to congratulate him on his victory, he'd already disappeared around the corner.

I found Chill tucked out of sight with his sketchpad in the far doorway of the school.

"That was cool!" I excitedly told Chill.

"No," he told me, coldly and firmly, looking up at me from his drawings. "It wasn't." He lowered his head, returning to his sketching. We never spoke of it again.

Well, *he* never spoke of it again. I told anyone who'd listen. I know violence is wrong, but that kid had it coming. Well, maybe not the six weeks on crutches and the endless teasing until he finally got a transfer—but still.

Chill got two weeks' suspension and was on probation when he got back, but that wasn't much of a problem. Chill never caused trouble, not real trouble, anyway.

The story—with as much help as I could give it—went through the school and the county, and by the time we got to high school it was told with the kid getting two broken legs—both broken in three places. Nobody bugged Chill about his leg again. That is, until the new teacher came. What

Chill did to that teacher would be a story to shadow the other one into obscurity.

It was the second year and the second semester of our four-year high school sentence, and we lucked out and got art for homeroom. I wasn't much of an artist, but it was an easy way to start your day if you didn't take it seriously and worry about things like color and contrast, light and shadow, lines and perspective—and I didn't. Chill did, though, so to get through I'd just mimic him as well as I could.

It's all right because in art it's not called cheating, it's called being heavily influenced by another artist. According to Chill, all the greats did it. It's like in film when everyone copied Tarantino after he copied the Hong Kong and Japanese directors. None of them were cheating or stealing. They were being "influenced by" filmmakers that they admired and respected. And I admired and respected Chill. (I also admired and respected Susie Jenkins' math skills, but we'll keep that between us.)

The teacher, Ms. Surette, couldn't tell that I was copying anyway. My projects looked nothing like Chill's no matter how heavily he influenced me.

Ms. Surette was the other reason that art was a great way to start your day.

There are three types of teachers. First, there are the teachers who just want to do as little as they can and go home. These are the ones who give you an assignment at the beginning of class that will take you the whole class to complete. They sit and mark work from their other classes so that they will have their nights and weekends free. They're easy teachers to have. As long as you're quiet, you can do just about anything you want with that hour—after you get the assignment done, of course. We'll call them type A.

Then there's type B. They're the ones who *end up* teaching, who think themselves better than it and are bitter at everyone for having to do this job that's so obviously beneath them. These teachers pick their favorites, who are always the students who are most easily controlled, and grind the rest down, crushing every dream you've ever had before the "real world" does it.

Type Bs are the ones who sparked the stereotype "Those who can't do, teach." They're not the majority, but they do the most damage, sticking with you as a little voice that cuts you down every time you dare think yourself worthy.

Finally, type C. Ms. Surette. A teacher who loves teaching.

A teacher who talks to you, not at you. A teacher who tells you that you can do whatever you want to if you put your mind to it. A teacher who understands that the "real world," which we're supposed to be frightened of, doesn't have wedgies, swirlies, people threatening to beat you up, constant put-downs and unbearable pressure from all sides to conform.

"If you can survive until university with just a little bit of yourself still intact, the 'real world' will be a much better place than the one you're in now," Ms. Surette said.

Ms. Surette was big on the "staying true to yourself" thing, which is why she liked Chill so much because Chill was Chill. She also liked him because he was a heck of an artist.

"Chill," she said, looking at his rendition of the bowl of fruit that she'd had us painting all class, "I want you to work on something else this semester."

"Sure," Chill said.

"You haven't heard what it is yet."

"That's okay," he said.

This made Ms. Surette smile. She had told us that when opportunities and challenges arise, saying yes opens doors; saying no closes them.

"Does that go for drugs too, Ms. Surette?" Pete Moss had asked. We had called him Pete since the time, for a dollar, he drank the water we rinsed our brushes in. It turned his teeth and tongue green for a week. His drugs comment got a small laugh from everyone.

"Yes," Ms. Surette replied, silencing Pete and the class. "The challenge and opportunity there is for you to show your willpower, your ability to think for yourself and not give in to the pressures around you. And to keep all your brain cells intact. And you should say yes to all those things."

"Yeah, Pete Moss, you don't have any brain cells to spare," I had said. The class laughed. Pete Moss showed me his IQ score by holding up a middle finger in my direction.

Ever since that day, Chill agreed to do whatever Ms. Surette asked of him, often before she could finish asking.

"Because," Chill said, "if she's asking it, it's going to be a challenge or an opportunity."

And in this case, it was both.

"The school is going to be doing a mural this semester," Ms. Surette told him. "I'd like you to design an entry, something that will inspire your fellow students. Are you interested?"

"Yes," Chill said.

"You'll be going against the seniors, but I think you've got a great chance if you work hard at it, and I know you will."

Chill humbly lowered his head while nodding thanks.

"You should do a self-portrait," I told him. He didn't hear me. He'd already taken out his sketchpad and started to work.

What he didn't know, what neither of us knew, was that his true inspiration had yet to arrive, but when it did, it would change the face of the school in ways no one could have foreseen.

Chapter Two

Second period was English. Because I wanted to be a writer I should have loved English, but I didn't. I couldn't understand why schools say that they want kids to read more and then make us study books that are guaranteed to turn any kid off literature for good.

They make us study the plays of a guy who's been dead for a few hundred years, written in a language that might as well be Klingon. If we rent the movie, it's considered cheating, which is ridiculous because plays were written to be performed and watched, not read.

The other books we're made to study don't have anyone near our age in them and don't take place in a time anywhere near our own. How can I relate to the 1930s when I'm still trying to figure out how to relate to the time I'm living in?

Replace Shakespeare with film study, poetry with lyrics, Steinbeck with Rowling—then maybe you might keep our interest. But we all know that's not going to be happening anytime soon.

Sometimes you'll get a teacher, one of those teachers like Ms. Surette, who finds a way to take the works of dead people and bring them back to life. Our English teacher was new to the school, and as Chill and I walked through the hall, nodding to the kids we hadn't seen since last semester, I hoped the new teacher would be just such a teacher.

"Have you heard anything about the new English teacher?" I asked Chill, who was sketching while he walked.

"Uh-uh," he mumbled.

"Maybe he'll be a teacher with a passion for the written word and pop culture," I dreamt out loud. "The mentor I've been looking for," I added.

"Yeah, maybe," Chill said as we turned into the class.

We'd discover—not soon enough—that he was not going to be my mentor, but Chill's muse.

Chapter Three

When we entered the room, the new teacher was nowhere in sight, just a briefcase sitting in the teacher's chair. I thought it was a good sign that the teacher was late. Maybe it meant he was a relaxed, laid-back kind of guy; the kind who would joke around with the students and be forgiving when they were late. This was not to be the case.

The teacher came in the door just as the bell rang. He was a big man. His shoulder-length hair covered his face as he walked with his head down. He carried a handful of books under his arm. His pale purple tweed jacket with pink elbow patches meant he was either totally out of touch or a little eccentric. I needed to see more before I could make a determination.

He turned to face the class, revealing a gray beard that masked his face and made it obvious that his hair was colored. The orange hair color that he'd chosen to help him hang onto his youth matched his bow tie. A bow tie!

"Crap," I said under my breath. "That's not good."

He glanced my way.

Fortunately, after years of practice, I'd mastered a speech level that most teachers couldn't distinguish, with any certainty, from the voices in their heads.

Mac Webble helped in my cover-up. Mac was a little guy to begin with, but he had been truly dwarfed by the teacher when he'd followed him in. Mac was trying to find a seat when the teacher noticed him.

The new teacher slammed his books onto the table.

"Boy standing!" he yelled.

Mac spotted a chair on the far side.

"Boy standing," the teacher repeated, picking up his books and slamming them down again.

Mac, realizing that he was the only one standing, looked around to be sure, then looked to the teacher and pointed to himself just to be absolutely certain, hoping to be wrong—a wish rarely made when called upon by a teacher.

"Yes, you," the teacher said slowly, as if he thought Mac was having difficulty with the language. "Why are you late?"

"Late?"

"Yes, that's what you call it when someone doesn't arrive on time. I see I've got my work cut out for me if you're any representation of the class's abilities."

"I followed you in."

"And I was right on time, which would make you…?"

"Late?" asked Mac.

"Very good," said the teacher. "Since we have made some progress today, I will let you take a seat and only put you on probation. If you're late again, you'll be going to the office. Now sit."

Mac stood for less than a second in fear and confusion.

"Now!" the teacher yelled.

This sent Mac stumbling over one desk before falling into another. He finally took his seat while rubbing his shin.

"Well, class," the teacher said, turning his back to us. He picked up a piece of chalk. "My name is…" and he sounded it out as he wrote on the board in big block letters.

"MR. S…F…I…"

He put extra emphasis on the *I*, making sure we understood that it was pronounced I, as in *I* hate my name. *I* will unleash a great wrath on any who mispronounce it. *I* still have nightmares over the locker it got me thrown into and the beatings *I* took. And then he quickly finished. "…NKTER."

As he finished writing *Mr. Sfinkter* on

the board, a collective snort went up as the class tried to hold back a giggle.

Mr. Sfinkter spun around, opening his mouth. There was a knock on the door.

The anger disappeared immediately and a wide smile crossed his face as he walked over to answer the door.

"Ms. Surette," he said, pouring on the false charm. "What a lovely surprise."

At the sound of her name, Chill looked up from his drawing. He had not heard or noticed anything that had gone on in the class to this point.

"And to what do I owe this unexpected pleasure?" Mr. Sfinkter asked.

"Chill forgot his bag," she said, holding up a knapsack.

"Chill?" he said and looked to the class.

"Chill?" he repeated with cheerful authority.

Chill raised his hand, identifying himself.

"Come and get your things."

Chill moved to get up.

"That's okay. I'll bring it to him," Ms. Surette said.

"As you wish," Mr. Sfinkter said, making a wide sweeping "come in" motion with his arm.

Ms. Surette smiled at his gentlemanly behavior.

Chill rose to take the bag from her.

"Thank you, Ms. Surette," Chill said.

"Let's try and not make a habit of it this semester, okay?" she said with a smile.

"I'll try," Chill said.

"That's all I can ask," she said and exited, thanking Mr. Sfinkter as he bowed to her and closed the door.

He made his way back to his desk, where he opened up his class list and ran his finger down it until finding Chill's name.

"Mr. Holinground, is it?"

"Yes," Chill replied.

"Should I expect you to be the cause of many interruptions?"

"No," Chill said.

"Good," he said. "And if you leave your bag in here, you may find yourself rummaging through the garbage bin to get it. Am I understood?"

"Yes, Mr...." and then Chill looked to the board, "Sfinkter."

Chill didn't pronounce the *I* as in *I* warned you, but the *I* as in *if* you show me respect, you'll get it in return.

"Sf*I*nkter!" the teacher yelled. "Or *sir* to you and everyone else for that matter! Since you all seem to have problems with the language, we'll use the small words!"

He was turning red, a red that, with his outfit, made him look like a demented clown. But after the narrow escape last time, no one snorted or giggled.

"Yes, sir," Chill quickly said, calming Mr. Sfinkter ever so slightly.

"For the rest of this class, I want all of you to write me a page on what you expect to do with your lives. That way, I can assess your English skills as well as your grip on reality. Now get to it!"

Chill took his binder out of his bag and went right to work with the teacher staring at him. As soon as he looked away, I saw a little smile cross Chill's face. I knew that this was only the beginning.

Chapter Four

The rest of the class was uneventful. Everyone worked quietly, trying to focus on their writing. I am sure we were all wondering what tortures lay ahead. I took a little solace in the subtle burn that Chill managed to lay on the teacher. It was things like that which made Chill popular with guys—his ability to get under a bad teacher's skin without ever taking it to a level to get in any real trouble. That and the story from elementary school where he broke the kid's leg in six places and fractured his ribs.

He wasn't popular like "going to all the parties" popular or captain of the soccer team popular. It was more of an "allowed to do what he wanted without a lot of ridicule from fellow students" popular. He got a lot of respect.

Chill knew he had that respect, and he gave that same respect to everyone. He wasn't a part of any clique; he talked to jocks and computer geeks alike. But I was his only close friend.

Girls liked Chill's confidence, but Chill was only interested in one girl—Sara Langdon.

Sara was awkward, clumsy even, but I think that was mainly because she always had her arms filled with books. She held the books tight against her chest and had an overloaded backpack over her shoulder.

She carried it all with her so that she could avoid her locker and hide out in the cafeteria or library. Her method of serving time in high school (and everyone needs some method) was to make herself invisible. And she was to everyone but Chill.

She was cute enough, in a plain, glasses wearing, bookworm kind of way, but I didn't see the attraction.

After completing my assignment, I looked over at Chill. He was watching Sara, who sat at the back in the seat closest to the door. I hadn't noticed her being there before that.

When the bell rang, Mr. Sfinkter told everyone to hand in their assignments.

I took Chill's up with me.

"You didn't say they were due at the end of class," Mac said.

"I'm saying it now."

"But, I'm not finished."

"Then you'll be starting the semester with an F."

"I can give you what I've got," Mac said.

"If it isn't finished, I don't want it."

"But…"

"But," Mr. Sfinkter mocked. "May I remind you that you are already on probation? I don't like to be pushed."

Then I heard the books fall. I didn't have to look to know they were Sara's. I also didn't have to look to know that Chill would already be there to help her pick them up.

Mr. Sfinkter did need to look. He sighed loudly and shook his head disapprovingly. Then he returned to the book he'd been reading all class.

Chapter Five

The afternoon was uneventful, filled with A-type teachers. Chill and I were in different classes. We met up after school and went to his place. We always went to Chill's because his mother worked evenings and wasn't home till 7:30.

Chill's mom, Orchid, worked as an anchor at the local television station doing the local news. She was a very driven woman, strong, from her long flowing brown hair to her perfect ankles…Ahhh.

Anyway, she'd read a lot of self-help books and had quotes hanging up all over the house like "See it, be it," "Believe and be," "Fear nothing," that type of thing. She'd post them, she'd read them, she'd follow them.

A few years ago, she had noticed that the local station didn't have a Crime Stoppers segment. She got a camera and got her husband at the time, Bill (a fool of a man for letting such a rare and precious flower go), to shoot re-enactments using local "actors." She announced the segments and starred in them a couple of times.

She was such a good actor that once people even called the police on her, thinking that the footage they saw was the actual crime. The police picked her up and took her to the station. It took a few hours to sort out, although, personally, I think the police just wanted an excuse to spend some time with her—and who could blame them?

The station soon took her on doing other reports, but they didn't hire her husband, and I think it was his jealously that brought about the end of the marriage.

She was sent out once to report on a local fire, but, always wanting to look her best, she stopped by her house to get a change of clothes. The way I heard it (as told by my mother to her friend while I happened to be crouched down just outside the kitchen door) was that when she arrived, she saw a car in the driveway that belonged to one of the "actresses" they had worked with in the re-enactments.

Orchid invited the cameraman to come inside. She made sure he was rolling when they entered the bedroom.

Orchid then proceeded to grab her change of clothing and take out a suitcase for Bill, telling him, "If you have your stuff out of here by the time I get home, I might let you keep some of it."

Then she went back to work and got the story. I think she may have even won an award for her coverage, but I can't be sure on that bit.

Chill still sees his dad every other weekend when his father makes the time, and Orchid tries to make sure that he does. "A boy needs a father," she says.

Orchid was a great mom, always encouraging and looking out for Chill—not that Chill needed any looking out for. That was why she didn't reveal her true feelings for me. I was sure that, when we went off to university, Chill would be old enough to handle it and she'd finally take me aside and confess her undying love. I was willing to wait.

Orchid went on to become a full-time news anchor at the station and selected any "field reports" she wanted to do, if she wanted to do any at all. We'd watch her every night—my day revolved around it. It was the only time I could freely enjoy her…everything. If Chill caught me enjoying when she was home, I'd get a very swift slap to the back of the head.

"What was that for?" I would ask.

He would only glare at me in return, not being able to say, "Stop checking out my mom," because to say it meant he was admitting his mom was worth checking out, and no guy wants to admit that.

She arrived home at 7:30, on the nose, every night.

"Hello, Ms. Holinground," I said with a welcoming grin.

"Hello, Sean," she said. She turned to hang her coat in the hall closet, unable to bear looking at me for fear of revealing her desire.

Whack!

"What was that for?"

Chill glared.

While most guys had an irrational fear of blindness from impure thoughts and deeds, I had a very real risk of concussion or severe brain damage. It didn't stop me, though, or even discourage me.

"How was your first day back at school?" Chill's mom asked.

"Fine," Chill told her.

"Our English teacher's a real jerk!" I said.

"Now why do you say that?" she inquired.

"Just is," I said, but then went on to elaborate on what had happened.

"Maybe you just need to give him a chance."

This was Orchid's one imperfection. She, like all adults, always took the side of the other adults, thinking that, as a teenager, I was prone to exaggeration.

"How was your day?" Chill asked her.

"Good," she replied. "They were asking about you at the station."

After his parents separated, Chill spent a lot of time at the station with his mom. He got to do all kinds of cool stuff like learn how to operate a camera, hang with local newspeople—who were celebrities in our little town. He even got to take a CPR course when the station paid for it. He never told me who he got to do mouth-to-mouth on, though—I imagine it was the woman who does the weather. If Orchid wasn't available to me, that's who I'd have gone for.

They also showed him how to put the composite sketches on video and would sometimes let him load them up for the "If you've seen this man" bit at the end of the Crime Stoppers segment that Orchid still introduced.

"You should come down to the station after school and say hello," Orchid suggested.

Chill just shrugged.

"I'll come down, Ms. Holinground," I volunteered. Orchid opened the fridge and reached for something on the bottom shelf.

Whack!

"What?" I asked, rubbing my head and looking at Chill. Chill glared back.

"Shouldn't you be getting home?" Orchid asked teasingly.

"My parents don't mind," I told her, to continue our banter.

"All the same, I think they'd like to see you," she said.

She does this all the time. When she thinks she can no longer contain herself in my presence, she casually asks me to leave. I show mercy.

"Yeah, I guess," I said, grabbing my bag. "Oh, yeah!" I added. "Chill's going to be doing the school mural!"

"Really?" she said. "That's great!"

"It's not a big deal, Mom," Chill said. "It's not even for sure."

"He'll be doing it, *for sure*," I confirmed.

"And when it's unveiled, I'll be there with a camera crew," she said. "It'll be the story of the year!"

Little did she know. Little did any of us know.

She kissed Chill on the cheek and gave him a big hug.

"I'm very proud of you," she said.

"Are you proud of me?" I asked.

"Yes," she replied.

I leaned in for my kiss.

"Go home," she said.

So coy.

Chapter Six

In art class the next morning, Chill already had a sketch of the proposed mural to show Ms. Surette. It had the school in the background. In the foreground were the faces of people like Pierre Trudeau, Wayne Gretzky, Albert Einstein, Shania Twain, Pablo Picasso, Mike Myers, Margaret Atwood, Alanis Morrisette…

"A mix of popular icons to inspire and encourage," as Ms. Surette put it. "I like it."

"And the quote?" she asked. "'The future is bright if you're not afraid of the light'—where's that from?"

"Sean," Chill quickly informed her.

I'd been inspired by Ms. Holinground and her many quotes.

"It's excellent," she told me. "I suppose you'll have to help with the mural too, then?" she said, more telling than asking. "I'll be making my decision at the end of the week. But it's safe to say that you have a very good chance."

"There won't be anything better," I told her.

"There's a fine line between confidence and arrogance, Sean," she said. "Best to stay well on one side of it."

Chill smiled. He had heard various people say the same thing before. He always found it funny. I didn't see the humor. It wasn't confidence or arrogance. It was pride in my friend's work. Since Chill never took much pride in it, always thinking he could have done better, I felt I had to make up for it.

"Anyone can do it," Chill said. "Most people just don't."

I didn't believe it. I knew I couldn't. Or I thought I couldn't. Maybe if I'd worked as hard as Chill—always sketching or reading about other artists, always working on something—maybe if I did that, then I could.

Chill even had a signature that he used just for his art, which was a work of art on its own, an unreadable symbol of original design. Maybe if I worked as hard at my writing as he did at his drawing…maybe it's just easier to think…

"Some people are just naturally good at things and others aren't," I said to Chill.

But in the back of my head I could hear Orchid saying, *If you put your mind to something, you can get it done, and don't ever let anyone tell you different!*

Chapter Seven

Mr. Sfinkter arrived in class just as the bell rang. He dropped his books on the desk and looked around at the class.

"Your essays were enlightening," he said. "Mr. Holinground?"

"Yes, sir," said Chill.

"You want to be an artist, do you?"

"Yes, sir."

"And how do you expect to support yourself?" asked Mr. Sfinkter.

"With my art, sir."

"You think that much of yourself, do you?"

"No, sir. But if I keep working at it…"

"Once that teenage ego of yours dies away, you'll realize that drawing is a hobby, not a career. Now would be a good time to start thinking about that."

"I'll take that under consideration, sir," Chill said while dismissing it.

"Well you can start by putting your doodling away and paying attention in this class."

"Yes, sir," Chill said, folding up his pad.

"I'd best not see that sketchpad again," he said, staring at Chill before he continued, "And Sean Fitzsimmons." I found myself immediately crossing my arms and legs. I felt like I was in one of those dreams where you show up at school only to realize that all you have on is your underwear.

"Yes, sir," I said, hoping someone would appear with a blanket for me to hide under.

"You dream of writing."

"Yes, sir."

"Well, perhaps you should spend less time dreaming and more time learning how to spell," Mr. Sfinkter said.

"Sorry, sir, my pen's spellchecker wasn't working."

I got a chuckle from the class, those brave enough anyway, but not from Mr. Sfinkter.

"And a smart mouth isn't going to get you far either!" he said angrily. He took a deep breath to compose himself. "If you want to be a writer, I would advise a teachers' college so that you'll have a job that pays while you write. It's very difficult to make a living writing, and I should know. I have three books published myself."

"Really, sir?" I asked with genuine interest.

"Don't sound so surprised," he said. "I have three works of non-fiction published, all about things that have happened to me in my life or to people I find worthy of my time and interest. Currently I am working on a fourth about all the authors and publishers that I have met, being in the business. I've had dinner with…"

And as he talked, the floor became littered with the names he was dropping. Some I knew, many I didn't. It was obvious by the way he spoke that I should be impressed. I tried my hardest to show that I was.

"You know, Mr. Fitzsimmons, if you are truly interested in becoming a writer, then you must write a book. Non-fiction is, of course, better, but that is best left to the more mature writers like myself.

"If you wish to show me that you're serious, then you must complete a work of at least one hundred pages, double spaced, twelve-point font. Spelling and grammar being, of course, the most important thing in those pages. If you do this, I will give it to one of my many publisher friends, who would be more than happy to do any favor I ask. In fact, if I think it's good enough, they'll publish it on my say-so alone."

"Really?"

"I do hope your writing is less repetitive than your speaking."

"Yes, sir."

"We'll see, won't we?"

"You'll give it to a publisher?" I said, unable to believe that such a thing could happen. I wanted to be a writer, but I thought it far out of my reach. And if Chill didn't have the talent to be an artist, I certainly didn't have what it took to be a writer.

"I am a man of words, Mr. Fitzsimmons," said Mr. Sfinkter, "so my word is my bond."

"Is that like a promise?" I asked.

"Yes, Mr. Fitzsimmons, that's like a promise."

He didn't read anyone else's career plans that day.

"I don't want to overload your developing minds, so we'll just do a couple of students a day. Give you all something to look forward to," he said.

And look forward I did.

Chapter Eight

I was no longer sure what to think of our new teacher. The chance he'd offered me was something beyond my wildest dreams.

Maybe he was just difficult because he thought that it was the best way to get us working. Maybe his outfits were eccentric and not a desperate cry for attention. Maybe there was more to him than I first thought.

Chill didn't like him. Chill didn't like anyone who trampled on other people's dreams, and that's what Mr. Sfinkter did at the beginning of every week. He'd take out two of the essays and go through them in front of the class.

It's embarrassing to have yourself exposed. It was obvious that everyone had the underwear dream that semester, but on top of revealing everyone's dreams to their fellow students, ensuring certain attack, he then provided the ammunition.

Mr. Sfinkter found fault with every career choice, picking them apart student by student. I got off lightly and was the only one who received the slightest bit of encouragement. Maybe it was because I wanted to be what he was.

Or maybe he saw something in my writing that he thought worthwhile. Whatever the reason, I took it and ran, starting to work just as hard on my writing as Chill did on his art.

If I could paint a picture with my words half as well as Chill could with a brush or pencil, I'd do great and Mr. Sfinkter would guide and teach me and make all that I could wish for come true.

I told myself that over and over again at the beginning of every class so that I wouldn't have to hear Mr. Sfinkter go on at the other students. But Chill, robbed of his sketchpad, had to listen to every word.

Chill's design for the mural was chosen as the best entry. Every morning throughout the semester, he and I spent first period working on the mural in the front foyer. When it was finished, it would be the first thing people saw when they entered the school.

There was little I could do to help him in the sketching part, which would take a couple of weeks. So I worked on my story while he did the mural outline. I kept a pencil close, and if we heard footsteps, I'd quickly get to work on one corner.

"What's it about?" Chill asked me.

"It's about a guy who everyone thinks is really mean, but he turns out to be a...it's about a lot of things," I said, not wanting to give too much away. Chill's feelings toward Mr. Sfinkter would probably cloud his judgment of my writing. Especially because the teacher had given me hope while telling

Chill he wouldn't be able to make a living from his art—despite his talents.

"When am I going to get to read it?" Chill asked.

"You're going to have to pay like everyone else," I said jokingly.

Chill smiled. He seemed to be as excited as me, or at least he tried to be, about the potential of my writing.

"Seriously, though, that's great that he's going to show it to publishers," I said.

"Can you take a look from back there and tell me if the ear looks okay?" Chill asked.

"I mean, even if he doesn't like it, he'll still give me input, and that's input from a published writer," I said.

"Does it look okay?" Chill asked.

"It looks fine," I replied.

"We should be able to start painting it tomorrow," he told me.

"Ms. Surette say anything to you about it?" I asked him.

"She said it was looking good."

"It's nice to get that encouragement from your teacher. Of course, you've always had it from your mom, so I guess to you it might not seem like a big deal," I told him.

"Sean, I..." he stopped. "You're a great writer no matter what he says about it."

"So you think he probably won't have anything good to say then?" I asked. It was obvious he was avoiding telling me what he really thought.

"I'm not saying that," he replied.

"What are you saying?"

"Just don't take anything he says too... be careful."

"Be careful?" I asked.

"That's all I'm saying," he said vaguely.

"Thanks," I told him, my anger building. "And you too."

"About what?" he asked.

"The mural," I said. "Not everybody's going to like it. And with it being at the front of the school, you'll have a lot of people taking potshots."

"I suppose so," he said, trying to seem indifferent.

"You know, saying it looks amateurish, asking what these people have to do with our school, saying you must be pretty full of yourself to think you, or anyone here, could ever be as good at anything as any of these people..."

"Sean..."

"I don't think that," I clarified. "I'm just saying what they might say, to prepare you. So be careful."

Suddenly the bell rang and I jumped to my feet.

"Don't want to be late for Mr. Sfinkter's class," I said, bolting.

Chapter Nine

As the semester went by, Chill and I talked less and less. Even when we worked together on the mural, I spoke to Chill only when necessary, to ask about a color or shade or which brush to use.

I began giving Mr. Sfinkter updates on how the book was coming, and he gave me long and impressive lists of all the people he knew. He told me how tiring it was when they were always after him to spend time with them and give them advice on their own works.

Mr. Sfinkter would only talk to me during class. It seemed that students were only visible to him during class time. We appeared when the bell rang and disappeared at the end of the period. It took a powerful mind to do that, the mind of a famous writer.

The more he talked, the dumber I felt for not knowing who he was when he first came to class. All his books were in the library. Well, they weren't when I first checked, but within a few days of his being at the school they were on the shelf. His website was filled with the wonderful things that he'd said and done and wonderful things others said about him. I couldn't find much else on the web about him, but I think that's because he was just so big he tried to avoid too much publicity.

You could see by the way he joked with and talked to the other teachers that they all liked him, even Ms. Surette. I think he was only teaching because he loved to share what he knew. Or perhaps he was just doing research for his next book.

As for his critique of the students' career choices, he was just trying to get us to look at things in a more realistic way, to prepare us for the "real world."

As the semester went by, I became certain that Chill's dislike for Mr. Sfinkter was simply jealousy and anger at the brutality of his honesty. Chill hated that I was getting the attention for a change. He was jealous that Mr. Sfinkter would let me work on my book but wouldn't let him work on his sketches. The day I finished the book and brought it into class was the day Chill's jealousy boiled over.

Chapter Ten

Chill and I ended up working behind a large tarp so that no one in the school would see the mural until it was completed. We were allowed to hook speakers up to my iPod as long as we kept it low. It made it easier to work without talking—less awkward.

"I've got to go," I told him one day.

"Where?" he asked. "The bell won't go for a while."

"I want to get to class early to give Mr. Sfinkter my book."

"You finished it? That's great!" he said with what could have been taken for genuine excitement. "Can I read it?"

"Yeah, sure," I told him. "I'll get you a copy when I get a chance."

"You can just e-mail it to me."

"Okay," I said, collecting my things. "Is it okay if I go?"

"Of course."

I started to get out from under the tarp when he called after me.

"Sean," he said.

"What?"

"Good luck."

"Sure."

Impatiently I waited at the front of the class for the bell to ring and for Mr. Sfinkter to appear. I think the rest of the class was there, although I didn't notice. I hadn't noticed them for most of the semester.

Mr. Sfinkter came in wearing a bright green jacket and red bow tie, his glory almost blinding me as he approached.

"Mr. Fitzsimmons, having trouble finding your seat?" he asked.

"I finished it," I told him, almost bubbling over.

"What did you finish?"

"The book."

"This is an English class, Mr. Fitzsimmons. You'll have to be specific as to which book you finished."

"My book, sir. The one I've been writing."

"What?" he said. "Oh yes, that. Good for you. I remember when I finished my first book. It was quite a feeling. My publisher was almost salivating when I gave it to him. The size of it alone was intimidating and struck him with awe."

He got taller when he talked about his book.

"But enough about me. We must get on with studying the works of my peers. Now take your seat."

"I have a copy for you, sir."

"You do? Oh, yes of course you do. Well, I can't very well read it now, can I? Set it on the desk and take your seat."

"You will read it, though?" I asked.

"Yes, yes," he said impatiently. "Now take your seat."

I set it gently on his desk before returning to my seat.

I sat down, twitching with excitement. I looked over at Chill. He seemed to be looking at me the way you look at someone who just received bad news, like their cat had died or something.

I couldn't figure out why at first. Then I figured that his jealousy had just turned to self-pity. I gave him a sympathetic smile in return. Maybe I'd been too hard on him.

"Well, thanks to Mr. Fitzsimmon's little delay, I'm only going to be doing one student's career today. And who's the lucky person?" He picked up my manuscript and tossed it in his drawer before shuffling through the last few papers and pulling one out.

"Miss Langdon," he said. "You want to be..." He quickly skimmed the paper. He laughed. "A doctor? Brains aside, with your clumsiness you'd be more likely to cause injuries than cure them. No, I think you'd best go for a rethink on that, perhaps picking a profession in which your work environment has no sharp edges. But nothing with small children, please. You'd kill them for certain."

I heard a snap and looked over at Chill. He was holding a broken pencil.

"Mr. Holinground, is there a problem?"

"None I wish to discuss," he said with the confidence and authority I used to admire.

They stared at each other for a while before Mr. Sfinkter finally spoke. "Good. Now everyone take out your copies of *Romeo and Juliet*. We'll be working on it for our final weeks," he said. "This play has a lot to teach you. It shows not only that children should always listen to their elders, but the dire consequences which result when they don't."

As we all took out our copies of Shakespeare, I saw Chill slip his sketchpad into his notebook.

For the first while he was doing a good job at covering up, looking up at the front and down to the pad as if taking notes on the passages that Mr. Sfinkter wanted us to pay the closest attention to. But as the class progressed, Chill's sketching became more frantic.

"Mr. Holinground," the teacher said. "Mr. Holinground!"

Chill dropped his pencil. "Yes, sir."

"It's nice to see you taking such detailed notes."

"It's a great play, sir," Chill replied.

"Despite what you may think, Mr. Holinground, I am not an idiot. Now bring your sketchpad to the front."

"Sketchpad, sir?"

"Bring it!"

Chill looked down at the sketchpad and then up to Mr. Sfinkter. I could only imagine what he'd drawn in his anger. I was sure it wasn't going to be complimentary to Mr. Sfinkter.

Chill took a breath. With his usual sureness, he got to his feet, sketchpad in hand, and started to make his way to the front.

"Pick up your feet when you walk, Mr. Holinground," barked the teacher.

At first, like everyone else in the class, I couldn't believe what I'd just heard. I knew that Mr. Sfinkter didn't notice us outside class, but could we really be that invisible to him?

The only one who didn't seem the least bit surprised was Chill. He kept moving.

"Pick them up!" Mr. Sfinkter repeated.

Chill stopped.

"I can't," he said.

"You *can't* or you *won't*?"

"I have a bad leg, sir."

"What do you mean by bad?" the teacher asked. "You sprained your ankle, perhaps tripping over that bag you leave lying around the school?"

"It's been that way since birth, sir."

"Oh," Mr. Sfinkter said, making it obvious that he'd just never noticed before now. "Well, I guess God's punished you enough then, hasn't he? Take your seat."

Chill spun around and returned to his chair without looking at anyone except Sara.

She looked at him without pity, without judgment, with just pure understanding. I realized then what Chill saw in her.

At the end of class, Sara took extra care with her books. Chill rushed out of the class, and I went after him.

"He didn't mean anything by it," I said.

"Which part?"

"About your leg, he really didn't know."

"What about Sara? And everybody else that he takes enjoyment in belittling, even you? You're just too…"

"I'm just too what?" I asked.

Chill shook his head. "I hope he helps you out, Sean. I hope he does all the things that he says he's going to do. But I can't turn a blind eye to all the things he's done."

And he walked away.

Chapter Eleven

All the way home I tried on different excuses for why Mr. Sfinkter did what he did. I needed a reason. I needed to believe that this man wouldn't be so cruel.

If he was really as nasty as he appeared, then what were all those people that he mentioned really like? Even the other teachers thought he was great. There had to be something more to him.

He did it to prepare us for the "real world," for things to come.

Once he did what he said he was going to do with my book, it would prove that he did want to help his students and not just put them down to build himself up.

By the time I got in the door, I'd made that excuse fit quite nicely. It had to fit. If it didn't, what would that say about everyone he'd told me about who looked up to him and were his close friends? What would it say about me, that I would defend such a person?

No, I thought. Whatever Mr. Sfinkter is doing, he's doing it for the best. Preparing us all for the disappointment that's bound to come in life.

At home that disappointment was everywhere.

Dad worked for a construction company and the only time he talked about his job was to bitch about the boss. Mom was a nurse and I always had to listen to her saying how useless most doctors were.

I hadn't told either of them about the book. There wasn't any point.

I went upstairs when I got home and read until 6:00, until the news came on. Now that I wasn't hanging out with Chill, it was the only time that I got to see Orchid, so I watched it even more religiously than before.

I was still thinking about what had happened in class that day when the Crime Stoppers segment came on. It was about a man suspected of flashing women in the west end of the city. The description was of a large heavyset man in his forties with a beard and bushy orange hair. A composite sketch of the suspect appeared on the screen.

Staring back at me was Mr. Sfinkter. My world came crashing down.

"It can't be!" I said out loud. "It can't be! How could he have fooled so many people? How could I have been so stupid?"

And then, just before the sketch left the screen, I saw, in the corner, Chill's unreadable symbol of original design.

"He's gone too far this time," I said. "He's gone too far!"

I paced the room, trying to decide what to do. Should I call the police? Should I call the television station? Should I call Chill? Should I call Mr. Sfinkter?

I went downstairs to where my parents were setting the table for dinner.

"I need to ask you guys something," I said.

"What's up?" Dad asked.

"Well…" I started, and I stopped.

"You see, Chill…" I tried again.

Mom stopped what she was doing and looked at me.

"Chill what?" she encouraged.

"Chill, he…"

I couldn't do it.

"Nothing."

"Well it must be something," Mom said.

"No, really, it's just a school thing. To do with a project. But I think I just figured it out. Thanks," I said and ran up the stairs.

"Hey," Dad called after me. "It's dinnertime."

"I'm not hungry," I yelled back.

For the rest of the night I sat in my room, staring at the ceiling, wondering what to do.

Chapter Twelve

The next morning it was all over the school.

"Did you hear what happened?" was the first thing out of everyone's mouth. I played dumb. Something that became increasingly easier to do.

"I heard he was arrested."

"I heard he's wanted across the country."

"I heard he's on a 'Ten most wanted list!'"

"I heard…"

I loitered outside the teachers' lounge to try and find out what had happened before I confronted Chill.

I heard Mr. Sfinkter's boisterous laugh. When I peeked in, I could see the teachers surrounding him, listening intently as he told a story about the whole ugly incident. They were obviously supportive, nodding sympathetically. Some offered comments, "…a terrible thing to happen…horrible…and to such a nice man…you should sue the station."

I thought I better find Chill. I went directly to the mural. Chill was already hard at work as if nothing had happened.

"I know it was you," I told him quietly.

"Could you hand me the blue?" he asked.

"It's not cool, Chill," I told him.

"You think the green would be better?"

"You know what I'm talking about."

He walked over and picked up the blue himself.

"I was going to call the station. I was going to call the police," I said.

"I heard Mr. Sfinkter was picked up and released," said Chill. "The station has no idea how it could've happened."

"They'll find out."

"If they do, they do," Chill said, shrugging.

"Why'd you do it on the day I handed in my book?"

Chill looked at me, confused. He shook his head and kept working.

"You know some people are still going to look at him like he's a flasher, whether he did it or not."

"He may not expose himself," said Chill angrily, "but he exposes every kid that comes through his class. Holding them up to ridicule and insult, highlighting every fear, exploiting every weakness and downplaying any good."

"That's not what he does for me."

Chill shook his head again. He looked at me with something like pity in his eyes.

"He's just preparing us for a world that you don't want to deal with. A world where everyone doesn't dote on you, encouraging your strong points," I said, looking at the mural, "while overlooking your weaknesses." I looked at his leg.

"Do you honestly think we can ever dream of accomplishing half of what these people did?" I said, pointing to the painted icons. "That's the reality that he's preparing us for. Maybe you should be thanking him instead of setting him up."

"And what reality is he preparing you for, Sean?" he asked.

Before I could respond, Ms. Surette called us from the other side of the curtain.

"Chill, Sean."

I went charging through the tarp. "Ms. Surette, can I return to class?"

"Is everything all right?"

I looked over at Chill, ready to spill it all.

"Everything's fine," I said instead. "It's just the finishing touches, and I'm in the way more than I'm helping."

"Is that okay with you?" she asked Chill.

"That's fine," he said.

"Okay then."

"Thank you," I said and left.

I'd just made the corner when I heard Ms. Surette say, "That was a strange thing that happened to Mr. Sfinkter, wasn't it?" I stopped.

"Yes," Chill said.

"I saw the drawing on the news last night. It was an incredible likeness."

Chill said nothing.

"I heard that the two of you don't get along," she said. She waited for Chill's reply. It didn't come.

"Anything you want to talk about?" Ms. Surette asked.

"No," said Chill.

"If there's a problem, I'd like to know about it," she said. It was obvious she wanted an explanation.

"He belittles everybody," said Chill finally.

"I haven't seen that."

"He's not that way with the teachers. It's when it's just him and the students that he shows himself," Chill told her.

"Maybe you should give him more of a chance. All I've seen is a very nice, charming man. Maybe you're misreading him or being a little oversensitive."

The silence hung heavier than the tarp. I leaned in to make sure I wasn't missing anything.

"Yes, Ms. Surette," Chill said mechanically.

I took some pleasure in hearing Ms. Surette reaffirm what I'd been trying to tell Chill. And myself.

"Good," she replied. "Now, can I see the mural?" she asked.

"I would rather no one saw it until the unveiling, if that's okay."

"Many great artists preferred to work in secrecy," she said. "That would be fine."

"Thank you," Chill said.

"But no more problems with Mr. Sfinkter, all right?"

"Of course," Chill said.

Chapter Thirteen

Mr. Sfinkter wasn't as jovial with the students as he'd been with the teachers. He was already in his seat when we arrived. He stared at Chill when he came in, his eyes following him to his seat.

After the bell, Mr. Sfinkter said nothing while the class sat in silence. He looked each one of us over.

"As I'm sure you've all heard," he began, "there was a bit of a misunderstanding last night. A local station, run by complete incompetents apparently—something that is reflected in their on-air personalities—ran a composite sketch of a man that looked a lot like me. It was an error." His eyes settled on Chill when he said this. Chill didn't flinch. "And they'll be apologizing for it," he told us.

"A lesser man than myself," he continued, "would hold a grudge and even sue the station and make sure that the employees in any way responsible would be fired." He again looked at Chill. This time Chill flinched. I knew it was the thought of his mom losing her job that did it.

"But I am not a lesser man. Children who are allowed to daydream become adults with sloppy work habits, and that station seems to be full of them. These people are to be pitied. For that reason, I'm going to forget about the whole thing and advise each of you to do the same."

And that was the last that was said about it, by anyone. Until we were out of class, of course.

Colin Frizzell

When the bell rang, I approached Mr. Sfinkter's desk.

"Sir," I said, "I was wondering if you had a chance to look at my book."

"What?"

"My book."

"I was a little busy last night, Mr. Fitzsimmons. When I read it, I will let you know. In the meantime, don't pester me or I'll toss it without a glance."

"Yes, sir," I said. Turning, I saw Chill at the back of the class, helping Sara with her books. I looked at Sara. She was smiling at Chill as if she was sharing in a private joke and promising not to tell.

I doubt that Chill told her about doing the picture. I doubt he told anyone. But word spread faster than poison ivy at summer camp, and this time without my help. Nothing could be proven because the sketch had mysteriously disappeared after airing. It seemed Chill couldn't really get into trouble, but among the students his popularity grew.

Chapter Fourteen

For the final weeks of the semester, we dissected *Romeo and Juliet*. We were shown that if they'd only listened to their parents, they'd have lived long, full and happy lives. Chill worked hard in isolation on the mural. Judging by the amount of paint that he was taking from the art room, there was more left to do than I thought.

I never asked Mr. Sfinkter about my book, and he never offered a report.

It wasn't until the second to last day of school, the day before the mural was to be revealed, that I approached him.

We'd been allowed to study in class as Mr. Sfinkter prepared the final examination.

After the dismissal bell rang, I approached his desk.

"Sir," I said.

"Not now, Mr. Fitzsimmons. I have work to do," he said.

"I was just wondering if you've had a chance to look at my book," I asked.

"Did you not hear what I said? I'm working."

"But tomorrow is the last day of school and you said you'd—"

"I said what?" he snapped.

"You said you'd read it, even give it to—"

"Here I am at work, preparing examinations for your fellow students, and you're bothering me over some whimsical promise I made months ago!"

He reached into the drawer that he'd set the manuscript in the day I gave it to him.

"Your arrogance in thinking that I would put your hobbies above my work and the needs of your fellow students has made any notes that I've made so far null and void! Your immaturity and complete lack of empathy show that you're incapable of writing anything of substance.

"Since these are traits that cannot be learned, I can tell you with all certainty that you are not now, nor will you ever be, a writer. Take your scribbles and get out of my sight."

My dreams drained from my body, leaving a shell that tingled with numbness.

"Now!" he yelled. I grabbed the manuscript and quickly exited.

As I made my way down the hall, I heard a sound behind me. I quickened my pace.

"Sean," Chill yelled. "Sean, wait."

I could hear his foot lifting and dropping as he tried to match my pace.

"Sean!"

I didn't stop. The only time I slowed was to toss the manuscript in the garbage.

I sat dead in my afternoon classes as the biology teacher rambled on about the Venus flytrap.

"Carnivorous plants have existed for thousand of years. The Venus flytrap attracts its prey with a sweet-smelling sap. The insect is drawn to it and then the jaws snap shut and the digestion process begins."

I tried to pay attention. I thought that maybe being a botanist might be more realistic than being a writer. But I couldn't focus.

When I left the school, I saw Chill going to the mural to do the finishing touches. He must have had special permission to work late.

The first thing I did when I got home was delete all my stories from my computer. It was time for a fresh start. I didn't know what I was going to start at. All I knew was it would be something more realistic than writing.

At dinner with my parents, I was still thinking about what I should do with my life.

"Mom, how long do you have to go to school to become a nurse?"

"You're thinking of becoming a nurse?" Dad asked.

"I don't know," I said.

"I thought you wanted to be a writer," said Mom.

"It's not very realistic is it?" I told them.

"Who says?" Dad asked.

"Everybody," I said. "Including you."

"When did either of us say that?" Mom asked defensively.

"You said it'd be hard."

"Hard," Mom said. "Not impossible."

"You never really encouraged it though, did you?" I said.

"We read your stuff all the time when you were younger," Dad reminded me.

"But you haven't recently," I replied.

"You haven't shown us anything recently," Mom said.

That was true.

"How are we supposed to show an interest if you never share anything with us?" Mom continued.

I wasn't sure how to answer. I was confused, to say the least.

"Well," I started slowly, "I wrote a book."

"A whole book?" Mom said. She seemed surprised and even proud.

I looked at Dad. He had the same expression as Mom.

"Where is it?" he asked.

"I threw it away," I told them.

"What? Why would you do that?" Mom inquired.

"I don't know," I said. At that moment I didn't know.

"Didn't you save it to your computer?" Dad asked.

"I deleted it."

"Well that wasn't very smart," Dad said.

"Calling him stupid isn't going to encourage him, dear," Mom said.

"I didn't say he was stupid. I said his actions were. And sometimes smart people can do dumb things."

I wouldn't have called myself a smart person at that moment, but I'd definitely have said that I did some *really* dumb things.

How would I ever make it up to Chill?

Chapter Fifteen

The next morning I received an e-mail from Chill before I went to school. He said that he had read my story and thought it was great. Attached was my manuscript, which he'd fished out of the garbage and scanned into the computer.

It should have made me feel better because it showed me not just that I had support, but that I'd been forgiven. But it made me feel worse.

It showed me just how great a friendship I'd turned my back on. It made me feel more foolish.

I printed off the manuscript and gave it to my parents. They seemed genuinely excited about reading it. I guess you could say that I was wrong about pretty much everything.

When I arrived at school, everyone was gathering in the foyer for the grand unveiling. We were supposed to go to our homeroom classes first and all go down together, but the last day is always chaos. Everyone knows you have to do something major to get in trouble.

As promised, Chill's mom was there—with a camera crew—looking as beautiful as ever. She smiled and waved. I smiled and waved back, but I still felt too guilty about Chill to enjoy it.

Chill was standing by Ms. Surette, holding the rope they'd hooked up to drop the tarp that covered the mural.

Behind them were the teachers, who also hadn't bothered to go to their homerooms.

In the center stood Mr. Sfinkter, telling his stories. I noticed that this time not all the teachers were listening to him. . Some stood apart, whispering to one another, often looking at Mr. Sfinkter as they did.

Chill waved me over, but I shook my head. This was his moment and I had contributed so little that I didn't want to be a part of it.

He moved toward me, but the bell rang. Ms. Surette grabbed his shoulder.

The principal took his place at the center of the curtain and got everyone's attention.

"I'd like to thank everybody for coming out this morning, particularly the members of the community, our local news station and our lovely local anchor, the mother of our featured artist," he said, gesturing to Ms. Holinground. Everyone, especially the boys, applauded.

"Although this was partially my idea, I want the proper credit to go where it's due, so without further delay, Ms. Surette, the head of our art department."

"Thank you, Mr. Gondale," Ms. Surette said, taking the floor. "And I must say, 'head of the art department' sounds much better than 'our only art teacher.'" This got a small chuckle.

"At the end of last semester, Mr. Gondale and I were looking at this large blank wall that welcomes all visitors to our fine high school and commenting that it was a very boring way to greet visitors. So, together, we came up with the idea of getting the students to design and paint a mural." This meant Ms. Surette came up with the idea but didn't want to show up the principal.

"I shared the idea with the students, to an enthusiastic response. There were many wonderful and creative entries. Unfortunately I could only pick one, and I felt that this one was the most representative of what we are trying to instill in the students here at Lakeside. But as Mr. Gondale said, I want to give proper credit where credit is due. Our artist, Mr. Chill Holinground," she said, handing over the floor.

Chill didn't move to center stage. With the turning of heads and thunderous applause, center stage moved to Chill.

Chill looked at the crowd. His eyes hesitated for a moment on Sara and then moved to me. "For all who dare to dream," he said, pulling the rope and bringing everything crashing down.

Chapter Sixteen

The mural had been changed. The basic elements were the same—a row of faces above with the school in the background. But the faces were no longer of famous people. They were the faces of a number of teachers, some with their backs to us, others looking up at a central figure who looked ominously down on everything. It was the face from the composite sketch, only this time he was in brilliant color, hair flaming. It was Mr. Sfinkter, the demonic clown.

Mr. Sfinkter's clothing looked more military than academic. He was wearing boots that were crushing Sara's and my heads. Beneath us, in Sfinkter's enormous shadow, were a variety of other students painted in black and white. I noticed that the school had bars on the windows and a fence surrounding it with spirals of barbwire at the top.

Chill had changed my phrase from "The future is bright if you're not afraid of the light" to "The future is bright if you don't get crushed by the darkness."

In the mural, Ms. Surette had an expression of confusion on her face, as if she knew something was wrong but didn't know what. In the corner by her feet was Chill's unreadable symbol of original design.

The group of teachers stood in silence. The assembled members of the community looked confused.

I looked at Chill's mom. She was staring at the painting. I was sure she was realizing what had happened at the station. She looked at Chill.

The students erupted in the loudest applause yet.

"Cover it up! Cover it up!" Mr. Gondale was yelling while grabbing the top of the curtain and lifting it.

It took a minute before some of the other teachers jumped in and assisted.

Mr. Sfinkter was standing off to the side. He looked very much like he did in the mural, only it was his face that was flaming, not his hair. His eyes darted about. I realized that he was being torn apart, not knowing what to do. He wanted to put on a brave face for the teachers, but his anger wasn't letting him.

When the curtain was finally up and covering the mural, the principal looked around. Chill was still standing where he had been when the curtain fell, his expression unchanged.

"You!" the principal yelled. He noticed the watching crowd and toned it down. "You, to my office, now."

Chill nodded as if everything was going as he'd expected it to go. He turned and started to walk toward the office.

"You too, Ms. Surette." Ms. Surette was still staring at the mural. It was as if she could see it through the curtain. Dazed, she looked at the principal. She nodded.

The principal quickly caught up to Chill. Mr. Sfinkter wasn't far behind, followed by Orchid and her camera crew. Ms. Surette looked at the wall again before following.

As I watched them disappearing down the hall, I knew that Chill wasn't going to slip out of this trick as he had all the others. I also saw that he'd accepted that fact.

The students had booed when they put the curtain back up and were now laughing and talking.

"He's going to get expelled for sure," I heard Mac say.

That's when I made my break for the lynch mob that was heading to the office gallows. I got there just before everyone went inside.

"I did it," I yelled.

They all turned around, including the camera.

"It was me." I hadn't thought this through. "I got into the school. I broke in last night. And I changed the mural."

I saw a vein in Mr. Sfinkter's forehead start to throb.

"Is he an abusive teacher?" the cameraman asked.

"Everyone in my office!" Mr. Gondale said before I could reply.

We all filed into the office. The principal stood at the door. He stopped the cameraman.

"Not you!"

"Freedom of the press!" the cameraman said.

"Just wait here, Don," Orchid told him.

"I can't let you in either," Mr. Gondale told Orchid.

"He's my son!" she firmly stated. "Now get out of my way!"

And he did.

Chapter Seventeen

They didn't care which one of us had done it. In their eyes, we were both guilty enough to be punished. Mr. Gondale and Orchid started venting immediately with simultaneous scolding.

The principal was ranting to all who wanted to listen and those who didn't.

"In all my years. I have never seen anything like this. There is no excuse," he babbled.

Orchid got involved too. She questioned his ability to run the school and accused him of not supervising his students or teachers.

But most of Orchid's shouting was focused at Chill and me.

The more people yelled, the calmer Mr. Sfinkter became. Ms. Surette stood in the corner, looking like someone had asked her a question she didn't know the answer to. Chill sat in a chair, listening intently but not saying a word.

I tried to defend us, but all I got out was "But...He...Well..." And eventually "Sorry."

"Sorry isn't going to cut it," Mr. Gondale said. "You're both going to be suspended immediately while we determine whether or not to take further action."

"What about our exams?" I asked.

"If you're allowed back, you'll have to do the semester over again."

A small smile crept across Mr. Sfinkter's face.

"What?" Orchid said.

"This school has a zero-tolerance bullying policy," Mr. Gondale said. "And they have to learn that there are consequences to their actions."

"What about his actions?" Ms. Holinground said, pointing accusingly at Mr. Sfinkter.

"I think Mr. Sfinkter is the victim in all this, wouldn't you say?"

"No, no I wouldn't say!" she yelled. "What we saw out there is the effect. I'd like to know the cause. And your 'zero-tolerance policy' should be just as stringent for teachers who bully as it is for students."

"That's insulting," Mr. Sfinkter said, no trace left of the smirk that he wore so proudly moments before. "How dare you accuse me—"

"Keep your bow tie on, Bozo," Orchid said, cutting him off.

I do love her so.

"All I'm saying is that there should be some kind of investigation before anyone is threatened with expulsion. The lack of one would not only be unfair, but it would look like the school was trying to cover something up."

"I can assure you, we're not trying to cover anything up, Ms. Holinground," the principal said in a patronizing tone.

"Tell it to my viewers," she replied.

As much as I would like to believe she was doing this for me, it was clear that Orchid was a bear protecting her cub. Judging by the look on Mr. Gondale's face, he'd just seen the length of her claws.

"I agree with Ms. Holinground," Ms. Surette said, having found the answer she was looking for.

"You," Mr. Sfinkter said. "You're to blame for all this, leaving these children unsupervised."

"First of all," Ms. Surette replied, "they're not children, Mr. Sfinkter. Secondly, I felt I could leave them unsupervised because they've never given me reason to distrust them."

"Now they have," he stated. The vein reappeared.

"And I'd like to know the reason for it," Ms. Surette said.

"This is ridiculous. They did it because I make them work for their grades."

"I think maybe..." the principal started.

"You're not actually considering letting them get away with this?" Mr. Sfinkter demanded.

"No one's getting away with anything. I just think it might be in the best interest of the school to further investigate before passing judgment," Mr. Gondale reasoned.

"You're joking!" Mr. Sfinkter said, his face bright red. "They're delinquents! And you're putting their word against mine! A respected teacher and author of four published books."

"Three, and they are self-published," Chill said quietly, breaking his silence.

Now, I had never checked who published the books; it's impressive enough that he wrote them. But judging by the way the vein on Mr. Sfinkter's head was pulsating, I'd say that not only was Chill telling the truth, but that he'd hit a sore spot.

"I will not have my reputation put in question by a mouthy little daydreamer and a gimp!"

The office fell silent. It was so quiet you could hear Mr. Sfinkter's mask shatter on the floor.

"I...I...I..." he stuttered. His stutters turned to gasps, then to a kind of choking sound. He grabbed his arm and collapsed to the floor like a bulk bag of gummy bears slipping off the storeroom shelf.

Chapter Eighteen

We all just stood there stunned as Mr. Sfinkter lay dying at our feet. I think part of our immobility came from shock, part from disbelief, and part from some dark little corner of our minds that thought it was for the best. But not Chill.

Chill dropped down, started to perform CPR and yelled to the principal to call 911, which snapped us all awake and we did what we could to help.

It seems that if you save someone's life, even if you're partially responsible for almost bringing it to an end, a multitude of sins can be forgiven. Chill and I were allowed to take our exams and complete the semester. Our punishment was to spend the first three weeks of our summer holidays restoring the mural to its original, approved, form. There was no iPod this time and no tarp, as the principal and Ms. Surette were by at least twice an hour to check on us.

After we finished, Chill had to do another month of "volunteering" down at the station for his Crime Stoppers stunt. His mom figured out what happened after seeing the painting, and though she didn't tell anyone else, she wasn't going to let him off no matter what the motive.

During that month the station manager saw some of his drawings and gave him a part-time job doing courtroom sketches. Then he got another with the police doing, you guessed it, composite drawings.

I was put under a month of parental house arrest and had to clean the garage and do all the yard work for the summer. Mom and Dad were both impressed by my book, though, saying that it showed a lot of promise. For my birthday they got me a new laptop, one gift certificate for our local bookstore and another for the stationery store.

There was never an investigation because Mr. Sfinkter decided to retire, saying that teaching wasn't his true calling. The last I heard, he was working on a book about his near-death experience and all the people that he'd met there in the light. They didn't want him to leave, but he knew his work on earth wasn't done—when it is his time, he apparently has an "in."

I didn't say anything to Chill for a while about everything that happened. Though he saved Mr. Sfinkter's life, he blamed himself for having to. Just like with that kid in elementary school, he'd never meant it to go that far. It was well into the summer before I finally brought it up.

"Chill?" I said.

"Yeah."

"What you did, it was cool."

"No," he told me, coldly and firmly, looking up at me from his drawings. "It wasn't," and then he lowered his head again, returning to his sketching, and we never spoke of it again.

Well, he never spoke of it again…

Colin Frizzell is an author, a poet and a screenwriter living in Toronto, Ontario. This is his first novel.

Other titles in the Orca Soundings series

Other titles in the Orca Soundings series

Visit www.orcabook.com for more information.

More Orca Soundings

Crush
by Carrie Mac

Isn't she fazed by any of this? Does she do this all the time? Make unsuspecting, seemingly straight girls squirm? Or am I making it all up? But making up what? The butterflies are real. The fact that I want to kiss her is real.

Would kissing a girl be different from kissing boys? If all I did was kiss her, would that make me queer? Are you queer just for thinking it? Or does doing it make you queer? And what if I don't want to be queer? Do I get a say in this at all?

Because of a moment of indiscretion, Hope's parents send her to New York to spend the summer with her sister. Miserable, Hope ends up meeting Nat and developing a powerful crush. The only problem is that Nat is a girl. Hope is pretty sure she isn't gay. Or is she? Struggling with new feelings, fitting in and a strange city far from home, Hope finds that love—and acceptance—comes in many different forms.

More Orca Soundings

Stuffed
by Eric Walters

"So, do we have a deal?" Mr. Evans asked.

"Unbelievable," I muttered under my breath.

"I don't understand," Mr. Evans said.

"The whole thing is unbelievable. First you try to threaten me. Then you try to bribe me. And now you do the two together, trying to bribe me and threatening me if I don't take the bribe."

"I don't like to think of it in those terms," he said.

When Ian and his classmates watch a documentary about the health concerns of eating fast food, Ian decides to start a boycott against a multinational food chain. Can Ian stand up for what he believes in? Can he take on a corporate behemoth and win?

Exit Point
by Laura Langston

"I'm not dead. I'm still me. I still have a body and everything."

"You are still you, but you don't have a body. What you're seeing is a thought form." He points to a tall gold urn up by the minister. "Your body is in there. You were cremated."

Thunk thunk, thunk thunk. My heart pounds in my chest. Dread mushrooms in my stomach. Sweat beads on my forehead. "But everybody knows death is the end. That there's nothing left but matter."

"Death is only the beginning, Logan. Hannah knows that. Lots of people do."

Logan always takes the easy way out. After a night of drinking and driving, he wakes up to find he has been involved in a car accident and is dead. With the help of his guide, Wade, and the spirit of his grandmother, he realizes he has taken the wrong exit. He wasn't meant to die. His life had a purpose—to save his sister!